REMNANTS: THE AWAKENING

By: Daniel Eakins

Published by Rust & Rebirth Press

First Edition – 2025

ISBN (Paperback): 979-8-9940058-0-4
ISBN (Hardback): 979-8-9940058-1-1
ISBN (eBook): 979-8-9940058-2-8

Cover and interior design by Daniel Eakins

For more information, visit
www.rustandrebirthpress.com

PREFACE

This story began in my dreams. Night after night, I saw fragments of a world that had fallen apart—pieces of cities half buried in dust, the sound of wind moving through hollow steel, and faces I didn't recognize but somehow felt connected to. Each dream picked up where the last had left off, as if the world itself was trying to show me what remained after everything else was gone.

What started as a recurring dream became something I couldn't ignore. I began writing down the moments that stayed with me: the broken machines, the flicker of hope in desolate places, the people searching for meaning when the world had forgotten theirs. Over time, those fragments became this story.

Remnants: The Awakening isn't just about survival. It's about the rediscovery of memory, identity, and the quiet strength that keeps us moving when everything around us has fallen silent. It is the first step into a world that wouldn't let me go—one that kept calling until I finally listened.

For anyone who has ever felt lost, or haunted by something too real to dismiss, this story is for you.

Daniel Eakins

ACT 1:
EMERGENCE

"The world around me was rust and smoke. I didn't know my name. I didn't know anything."

Chapter 1

The Awakening

I woke to the sound of breathing that wasn't mine.

The air smelled of ash and oil, heavy enough to sting the back of my throat. When I pushed myself upright, my hands scraped against rough concrete, gritty and cold beneath my palms. A dim light flickered overhead. It pulsed like a dying bulb, revealing fragments of the room: rust streaks on the walls, dust drifting in the air, shadows that shifted but did not move. My eyes burned as I tried to focus. I was too weak to see

clearly, but clear enough to know I was not
alone.

A girl sat pressed into a far corner, watching
me with wide, unblinking eyes. She looked no
older than twelve, small and thin, her knees
hugged tight to her chest. She did not speak. She
did not move. Her skin was pale beneath the
grime, her frame wiry, like someone who had
lived hungry long enough for it to shape her.
There was something almost familiar about her
face, but the thought slipped away before I
could grasp it.

Two men stood several paces behind her.
Both silent. Both staring. One was tall and thin,
shoulders slumped, his face swallowed by

shadow. The other was heavier, arms crossed tight as if bracing for trouble. No one spoke.

I tried to ask where we were, but my throat refused to form sound. My tongue felt swollen, my mind frayed at the edges. I hadn't forgotten everything. I remembered enough to know something was terribly wrong. But whatever had brought me here was lost inside a fog I could not push through.

Somewhere deep in the distance, machinery began to stir. A low groan rolled along the floor, followed by a sharp hiss and the clatter of gears. The sound filled the hall like distant thunder.

That was when I noticed the absence of doors. No windows either. The place stretched farther than the light could reach, an endless industrial chamber of smoke and shadow.

A voice rose suddenly through the noise.

At first it sounded like rambling, a man speaking far off in the dark. His words tumbled out in a frantic stream, breathless and uneven. For a moment it seemed like nonsense, but the longer he spoke, the clearer the edges became.

"They are watching. Eyes in the smoke, eyes in the wires, eyes even in the puddles when the rain comes. Suits in the towers drinking the oil from our bones. They smile, but the teeth are not theirs. Do not wave at them. Do not smile back."

The girl's head snapped toward the sound.

One of the men whispered, "Shut him up before they hear."

But the voice kept rising, sharper, desperate.

"She walks among us, cloak like smoke, hands full of gifts. Not for you. Not for me. For the chosen. Always the chosen. We are sparks in the ash, waiting to burn out."

A shiver crawled down my spine. His words meant nothing to me, yet they dug under my skin. The machines groaned again, drowning him out. When the noise dipped, he was still talking.

"They took your life. Scraped it clean. Left you hollow. The pictures in your head are not yours but theirs. They let you work and bleed, but they will not let you remember. Not until the end.”

The girl pressed closer to me. Her small fingers clutched my sleeve, trembling through the fabric. Her gaze stayed locked on the smoke as if she could see shapes moving inside it.

When she finally spoke, her voice was a thin whisper. “They will hear us if we stop.”

I opened my mouth to ask what she meant, but she shook her head with quick, frightened urgency. My tongue fumbled over a stray question that made no sense even to me.

“What is the… infrastructure here?”

She blinked in confusion, unsure what I had said. Before either of us could speak again, the machinery roared to life, swallowing everything.

And then the work began.

Chapter 2

The Workhouse

The girl's warning echoed in my mind as the machinery roared to life. The floor vibrated beneath my feet, a steady pulse that matched the hiss of steam and the grinding of gears. Around us, the others moved without hesitation. They already knew the routine. They already knew the rules.

I did not.

My body felt heavy, my thoughts thick with fog. The two men who had been standing beside the girl drifted into the haze without a word, swallowed by smoke until only the crunch of their boots proved they had not vanished entirely.

The girl tugged at my sleeve and pulled me forward.

A sharp pressure built behind my eyes, sudden and jarring. It felt like a memory clawing its way out of a locked room. For a moment the yard dissolved. The clanging machines and hunched bodies flickered away, replaced by a tall room of glass and steel. The air there was bright and cold, and a line of faces stared at me with something like expectation.

Then it disappeared. Just the yard again. Gray. Loud. Choking.

I pressed my palm against my brow as the ache burrowed deeper. Something inside me wanted to break free.

The overhead light shifted into a weak yellow glow that barely cut the fog. That was when I saw the work lines. Long tables stretched into the darkness, covered with piles of metal scraps, coils of wire, and shards of broken glass. Men, women, and children worked with bare hands, fitting pieces together, hammering, twisting, welding. No guards shouted commands, yet everyone moved with a rhythm that felt carved into their bones.

The girl sat, and I followed her lead. Across from us a man worked in silence. His beard was stained dark with grease, his skin pale, his eyes hollow. He never acknowledged me. His hands moved on their own, snapping two jagged plates together with a riveting tool that looked older than he was. The scraps he handled looked useless, shapes of rusted steel with no purpose I could name, yet he kept reaching for more.

The girl's movements were quick and sure, sharper than her thin frame suggested. She handed me a strip of copper wire. I threaded it through a hole in the metal plate she pushed toward me. My hands trembled. Hers did not.

Above the drone of work, the rambling man's voice carried. Louder now. Closer.

"They are watching. Eyes in the smoke, eyes in the cracks. The ones in the towers drink your sweat like wine. They smile when you bleed. They cheer when you break."

The bearded man across from us clenched his jaw. "Shut him up," he whispered. Fear trembled beneath the words. "He'll get us all killed."

No one moved to silence the rambling man. His voice flowed on, blending with the hum of the machines.

"She walks among us, cloak like smoke, gifts in her hands. You will see her when you have lost enough to want her."

The girl twisted the wire in her grip until her knuckles turned white. She kept her head down and her hands moving.

I leaned closer, keeping my voice low. "What are we making?"

Her eyes flicked toward me for a heartbeat, then away.

"Do not ask," she whispered. "Not yet."

Even the machines couldn't drown that warning.

The rhythm of the work stirred another echo inside me. A faint memory of polished boots striking marble. A hall full of chanting voices. The flash of a symbol I could not name. I blinked hard until it dissolved, thinking it was only exhaustion.

What is this place? Why can't I remember anything?

I forced my hands to match the girl's

movements. Piece after piece. Wire after wire.

Time smudged at the edges until I could not tell

when the work began or when it might end.

CHAPTER 3
THE RAMBLING MAN

The shift ended in a wash of steam and sweat. My hands shook from the constant vibration of the machines, every bone aching as though I had been working for weeks rather than hours. The crowd of workers shuffled toward an opening that resembled a gate, silent as always, heads low and eyes dull.

That was when I heard him.
A voice cutting through the monotony, sharp and cracked.

"They see you. Every second, they see you."

I turned, expecting someone to silence him, but no one did. The workers kept moving, treating his words like part of the noise that haunted this place.

He stood apart from the line, a gaunt old man with a wiry beard and bloodshot eyes. His clothes hung from him in tatters. His fingers twitched as he pointed toward the towering machines.

"You think it's the overseers. It's not. It's the Eyes. Always the Eyes. Watching. Listening. They record every breath you take. They chew up every thought in your skull."

The girl tugged my arm. "Don't. Keep moving."

But something in his voice pulled me in.
Something wild. Something familiar. The old
man's gaze locked on mine, and for a heartbeat I
could swear he knew me.

"You hear it, don't you?" he said. He
staggered closer, breath thick with rot. His
words tumbled too fast. "Prime is still
humming. The whispers in the gears. They talk
when you are alone. Telling you to work. Telling
you to obey. Don't you hear it?"

A pulse. A presence. A dull throb beneath the
machinery.

I swallowed hard. "I don't know what
you're talking about."

He laughed, dry and broken. "That is how it starts. You deny it. You push it down. Then they slip inside. Until all you are is another drone."

The girl stepped between us, her voice sharp. "Enough. He is new. Stop filling his head."

The old man sneered at her, spit flying. "New or old, it makes no difference. The Eyes don't care. The city remembers. It always remembers." His gaze swung back to me, burning with a feverish conviction. "Don't sleep with your face uncovered. They crawl in through your eyes."

Before I could respond, his hand clamped around my sleeve. His grip was surprisingly strong, cold and desperate. My pulse spiked. I yanked free.

"What is wrong with you? Are you insane?"

He threw his head back and laughed again, a sound frayed and hollow, then staggered off, muttering about wires under the skin and a darkness that watched from behind the walls. The workers gave him a wide berth, but none spared him a glance. His madness was part of the landscape here.

The girl exhaled slowly. "Ignore him. He is broken. Too long in the yard does that to people."

I wanted to believe her, but his words clung to me like grit in an open wound.

The Eyes.

The whispers.

The machines that felt alive.

That night, lying on the cold ground, I pulled the thin blanket over my head and closed my eyes tight.

I wasn't sure what I feared more: seeing something in the darkness or remembering what he said I had forgotten.

Chapter 4

Shadows Among the Shifts

The next day the machines stopped without warning. One moment the floor trembled under the weight of gears and hissing steam, and the next it fell silent. No horn. No bell. No voice calling the end of a shift. Just stillness, sharp and sudden.

Everyone around me froze, their hands suspended above their work. Metal tools clattered to the tables. Scraps lay half assembled. Then, as if bound by one thought, the workers stood and formed a slow-moving line toward the far end of the hall.

I rose with them, unsure if I was supposed to follow, but the girl had already taken my sleeve. "This way," she whispered.

We walked with the crowd. As we moved, the smoke thinned, revealing rusted pillars that rose into a ceiling swallowed by shadow. It felt like walking through the ribs of a dead giant. The air tasted damp and metallic, heavy on my tongue.

At the edge of the hall the workers broke into clusters. No voices rose above a murmur. The two men who had been with us when I first woke were nowhere in sight.

I scanned the hall. "Where are they?"

The girl shook her head slowly. "People don't always come back."

"Back from where?"

Her silence did more damage than any answer would have.

We pushed past the clusters into a narrow corridor where the ceiling dipped low and the air cooled. For the first time since I arrived, I felt a breeze. When we stepped out of the corridor, a pale light hit my eyes.

It wasn't sunlight, not really. The sky above was a washed-out gray behind haze, but it was brighter than anything inside. Before us stretched a courtyard of cracked concrete and broken ground, ringed by rusted wire fences and leaning posts. Workers drifted through it in weary silence, collapsing against walls or curling into corners as if sleep might catch them where they fell.

"What is this place?" I muttered.

"How does anyone stay here?" I asked.

"They don't have to," the girl said. She knelt to pick at a weed pushing through a crack, her casual gesture as telling as any explanation.

I looked at the fence. Rust had eaten through half the wires, leaving gaps wide enough for anyone to slip through. Beyond the fence lay a dirt road stretching toward jagged hills. Nothing stopped anyone from walking out.

"Then why stay?"

Her gaze shifted to a huddle of workers near the far wall. A man whispered frantically while another spat in disgust. "The Rustclads will gut him before nightfall," the worker muttered.

The word cut through the air like a blade.

The Rustclads.

I stepped closer to her. "What are they talking about? Who are the Rustclads?"

Her face went pale. In that moment she looked younger, her bravado stripped away.

"They wait outside the yards," she said finally. "They take anyone who leaves. If you're lucky, you die fast."

"And if you're not lucky?"

She didn't answer.

The yard emptied as people found corners to collapse in or hide. Others whispered about the hills or the watchers in the dark. Every mention of the Rustclads carried tension like a pulled wire.

"Not the first time the Towers made someone disappear," a worker muttered as we passed. He shut his mouth quick when he realized I had heard him.

I scanned again for the tall man and the heavy one. If they had slipped through the fence, they should have been somewhere on the road. But the dirt stretched into haze without footprints. No tracks. No bodies. Nothing.

The girl tugged my sleeve and guided me toward a shadowed corner where the walls curved inward. We sat on the cold ground with our backs pressed to stone.

"Rest," she murmured.

Questions clawed at me, but exhaustion dragged heavier than fear. I closed my eyes as whispers drifted around us.

The Rustclads are waiting.
The Rustclads are always waiting.

I tried to sleep, but one truth pressed deeper than the whispers.

Something had happened to those men.

And it had happened fast.

Chapter 5

Empty Places

The yard was quieter than the work hall, but not by much. The machines were gone, yet the silence felt heavier, crowded with things no one dared to say.

Clusters of workers hunched in corners, speaking in low voices, their eyes darting toward the broken fence as if expecting something to crawl through it at any moment. Smoke drifting from the factory clung to everything, staining the air and smothering even the faint gray sky.

The girl leaned against the wall beside me, her knees pulled tight to her chest. She seemed smaller out here than she had at the tables, as if the open space weighed on her more than the constant pressure of the machines.

I scanned the yard again, searching for the two men who had been with us when I woke. The tall one. The heavy one. Still nothing. Not in the corners. Not among the clusters. No trail in the dirt. Gone as though they had never existed.

My stomach twisted.

"They didn't just walk away," I said.

The girl didn't answer.

A sharp voice cut across the yard. An older man hunched near the fence whispered to the group beside him. His eyes were wide and feverish, his hands trembling against his knees.

"They took a boy last night," he said. "Slipped right through the wire. Thought he was free. By morning they found his boots empty in the dirt. Just the boots. Nothing else."

The group murmured uneasily, but no one challenged him. A woman nearby shook her head. "Stories. That's all."

The old man's voice cracked. "You think they are stories? You think the Rustclads don't wait out there? They are always watching. They don't let anyone leave."

I shifted closer to the girl. "Is it true?"

She didn't look at me. Her eyes stayed fixed on her knees, her arms wrapped tight around herself.

"I told you," she said softly. "If you are lucky, you die fast."

The words slid coldly into me. I wanted to press her, wanted to demand what she had seen or heard, but the way she stared at the ground told me enough. She wasn't repeating rumors. She was remembering something.

Another cluster of workers nearby argued in hushed whispers.

"They're not real."

"They are real."

"Then why don't we ever see them?"

"Because they see you first."

The whispers drifted through the smoky air, each one feeding the next until the yard seemed to hum with the fear of unseen eyes.

I turned back to the fence. Holes gaped wide enough to crawl through. The road stretched out empty, but the emptiness itself felt like a trap. The kind of silence that waits for you to believe it's safe.

The girl tugged my sleeve, her voice tight. "Don't look too long. They notice."

"They?" I asked.

Her grip tightened. She didn't answer.

The yard settled into an uneasy quiet. Clusters broke apart as workers curled into sleep or stared hollow-eyed into the washed-out distance. Exhaustion pressed down on me, but my thoughts kept circling back to the missing men.

Two shapes. Two breathing bodies. Now nothing. Whatever had happened to them had happened fast.

Wind whistled through the ruins, carrying a sound like a warning. It cut through the shells of what must have once been a thriving community, now reduced to dirt, rust, grease, and dread.

For a moment, as the wind howled through the wreckage, I saw something else. Clean stone. Rows of officials in pressed coats. Myself standing above them.

A single word surfaced:

Reform.

The image vanished as quickly as it came,

leaving only rust and dirt.

"She left without a word. The silence she left behind was heavier than before."

Chapter 6

The Cloaked Woman

The yard had fallen into uneasy stillness. Workers slumped against the walls or curled into the dirt, too hollow to speak, too exhausted to dream. Wind slipped through the ruins, tugging at scraps of cloth and rattling loose sheets of rusted tin.

The quiet pressed down hard, heavy enough to swallow us whole.

I must have drifted off, because when my eyes opened again, the girl was shaking my shoulder.

"Wake up," she whispered.

I followed her gaze.

Then the rumble came.

A low vibration stirred beneath the ground, faint at first, then building into a mechanical growl. I pushed myself upright. Around us, others stirred as well, shoulders tightening as their eyes flicked toward the gaps in the fence. Even the girl drew closer, her small hand tightening around my sleeve.

Through the haze, a shape emerged. A tall-sided vehicle, paint stripped and metal dented, rolled to a stop just beyond the wire. Smoke coughed from its exhaust, drifting upward into the gray sky.

The door creaked open.

A figure stepped out, draped in a cloak that shimmered like ash in the wind. Her hood was drawn low, hiding her face, but the air seemed to shift around her, tightening with every step. Workers reacted to her presence in ways I didn't understand. Some lowered their heads. Others stared with a strange mix of fear and longing.

For a moment I thought she was part of the smoke itself. Her cloak hung heavy, black or dark gray, its edges curling like mist. She moved with slow, deliberate steps. The hem brushed across the cracked concrete.

Whispers followed her.

"It's her."

"She's here."

"The woman in the smoke."

The girl pressed close to me. "Do not let her see you staring."

Workers lowered their eyes, some turning away entirely, as though looking at her was enough to invite punishment.

"Who is she?" I asked.

The girl's voice tightened. "The one he spoke about. The one with the gifts."

The rambling man's voice echoed in my mind. The woman in the smoke. The one who brought gifts for the chosen.

The cloaked woman approached a broken van. From within her cloak she drew three items and placed them carefully on the windshield: a folded newspaper, a brown-wrapped package the size of a loaf of bread, and a carton of ice cream, pale against the grime.

I could not breathe. Something in her presence pressed down on me, heavy and suffocating yet impossible to turn away from.

The girl trembled beside me.

The woman lingered only a moment longer, then turned. Without a word or a backward glance, she stepped into the vehicle again. The door slammed shut. The engine coughed, growled, and the vehicle rolled away, swallowed quickly by the haze.

The silence she left behind felt heavier than before. I stared at the windshield.

Who had that kind of power? Who could silence an entire yard with nothing but their presence?

Then the old man appeared.

He burst forward from the shadows with startling speed, a hunched figure draped in rags, beard matted with grease and dirt. His eyes were wild and darting, as though expecting someone to strike him down.

He clawed at the windshield, snatching the newspaper and the package, cradling them tight against his chest.

But he left the ice cream.

"Mine!" he shouted, voice cracking. "Mine, not theirs. Not theirs to take."

He staggered back, muttering to himself, fragments spilling from his mouth like broken glass.

"They took them, you see them no more. The tall one, the heavy one. Gone like the rest. Boots empty, eyes empty, nothing left but bones in the smoke."

His eyes met mine, wild and knowing. "I have seen your kind. Shouting from the Towers, promising change. And now look at you."

The girl tugged my sleeve sharply, whispering, "He's raving. Ignore him."

But my stomach dropped.

The old man's words clung to me, sharp and jagged. The tall one. The heavy one. Gone.

He melted into the shadows at the far wall, curling around his treasures like a dog guarding a bone. No one stopped him. No one asked. It was as though he had already ceased to exist.

I looked back at the windshield. The ice cream sat where he left it, condensation beading along the sides, a pale trickle running down the glass.

Untouched.

No one moved toward it. No one dared.

"What did she give him?" I asked.

The girl shook her head slowly. "Some things are not meant for us."

The ice cream continued to melt, a pale streak in a world of rust and dirt and dread.

And with it came the crawling certainty that the cloaked woman had not brought gifts.

She had brought warnings.

Chapter 7

Fractured Bonds

A few days passed in a blur. Each evening the yard emptied into shadow as the last of the workers slumped against the walls. Smoke drifted low and caught in my throat. The machines were quiet, but their echoes still rang in my ears like phantom chains.

The girl and I sat in our usual corner, backs pressed against cracked stone. She kept her knees pulled tight, her chin resting against them, eyes fixed on the dirt. I stared at the place on the windshield where the ice cream had melted into a pale streak, a clean line in a world built on decay.

I broke the silence first.

"What was with that mysterious woman the other day?"

Her shoulders tensed, but she didn't answer.

"The woman," I pushed. "The cloak, the things she left behind. Everyone acted like they saw a ghost. Maybe they did."

Finally, she whispered, "She is not for us."

"What is that supposed to mean?" My voice came out harsher than I intended. "You saw it too. A newspaper. A wrapped package. Ice cream. Here, of all places. Tell me that's normal."

She lifted her head. Her eyes caught the faint gray light, older than she was, sharpened and worn down at the edges.

"Normal died a long time ago," she said.

I let out a bitter laugh. "That's comforting."

She turned away, hugging her knees tighter. Neither of us spoke for a long time. The wind pressed through the holes in the fence, whistling low, as if it carried voices we were not meant to hear.

When she finally spoke again, her voice was almost too soft. "Do not look at her. Do not want anything she leaves behind. That's how you stay alive."

I studied her in the dim light. Beneath the dirt and wiry frame, she held a stubbornness that belonged to someone who had clawed her way through hell and kept going, even if only barely.

"You talk like you've seen her before," I said.

Her silence was answer enough.

"She leaves things behind to see who takes them," Nora said. "Food. Water. Trinkets. It does not matter what. She watches from the ruins. If someone reaches for the gift…" Her throat bobbed. "She marks them."

"For what?" I asked.

Nora wrapped her arms tighter around herself.

"For being weak."

I leaned back, letting my head rest against the stone. "You know, I do not even remember who I was before this. I woke up in that room with you and those two guys, and it's just blank. Like my whole life got scraped out."

She shifted, watching me from the corner of her eye. "Maybe that is a mercy."

Her words hit harder than I expected. "You really believe that?"

She shrugged. "Maybe what is out there isn't worth remembering."

"Sometimes I get flashes," I said quietly. "Crowds, speeches, men in fine coats. I do not know if it is memory or something my mind invented. But it feels real."

She studied me for a long moment, then looked away. "Don't chase ghosts. It will get you killed."

I wanted to argue, to tell her she was wrong, that maybe I once had something worth remembering. But the truth was I did not know. I had nothing. No name. No past. Just this place, this moment, and the girl beside me.

For a while we sat in silence, listening to the wind. Workers drifted into shallow, uneasy sleep around us, their breathing rough, their bodies twitching as though fighting unseen battles in their dreams.

The girl rested her head against her knees. Her voice came muffled. "If you are smart, you will stop asking questions."

"And if I am not smart?" I asked.

She lifted her head just enough to look at me. For the first time since I met her, a trace of something almost like a smile tugged at her mouth.

"Then you will end up like the others."

The smile vanished as quickly as it came, and her eyes drifted shut. Within minutes her breathing slowed and steadied. She slept against the stone.

I stayed awake longer, staring at the dark fence and the holes that opened into nothing but smoke. My thoughts circled the old man's warnings, the missing men, and the shadow of the cloaked woman. And somewhere beyond the ruins, something waited for us.

ACT 2:
THE ENCROACHING THREAT

"*They say The Rustclads don't just take you. They keep you.*"

Chapter 8

Whispers of The Rustclads

The yard never really slept. The machines slowed, but they never stopped. Even in the dead hours, their groaning, grinding hum threaded through the rust and stone, a pulse beating against your skull until silence felt like something forgotten.

But that night felt different.

Workers gathered in clusters, speaking in hushed voices. Not the usual muttering about shifts or broken tools. Something darker. Their eyes kept darting toward the fences, toward the shadows stretching beyond them.

I sat against a wall, my body aching from another brutal shift. The girl sat close beside me, her arms wrapped tightly around her knees. She did not join in the whispers. She never did.

"They take them at night," one man whispered, his voice cracked like old leather. "Not the overseers. Not the yard. Them. The ones outside."

Another worker snorted. "Nonsense. It's the yard itself. Swallows them whole. You have seen it. Tools dropped mid-swing, boots left behind."

"No," the first man snapped. He spat into the dirt. "I heard them. Laughter out in the dark.

Saw fire burning on the horizon. They are waiting. Watching."

Someone else leaned in, their voice trembling. "They eat the ones they take Strip the flesh. Hang the bones like warnings."

A sharp hiss cut through the group. "Fool. They do not eat them. They work them. Drag them back to the ruins, chain them up, make them build their empire."

The arguments blended together. Eating. Enslaving. Vanishing into nothing. Nobody agreed on the details, but the fear was the same. It hung thick in the air, heavier than the smoke, thicker than the stink of sweat and oil.

I glanced at the girl. Her face revealed nothing, but her hands dug into her knees until her knuckles went pale. She had heard these whispers before. Too many times.

I leaned closer. "Do you believe any of this?"

She didn't look at me. "It doesn't matter what I believe. It matters what's waiting for us if it's true."

Her words stayed with me long after the group broke apart and the murmurs faded. The machines groaned back to full strength, drowning out their voices but not the unease that had settled deep in my chest.

When I finally lay down, the images refused to leave me. Fires on the horizon. Laughter in the dark. Hands dragging the missing into places we couldn't see.

Chapter 9

Tempting the Outside

The yard felt smaller with each passing shift. Same fences. Same rusted scaffolds. Same blank faces slumped against the walls at night. It was a cage, and I could not stop thinking about what waited beyond it.

That night, when the machines finally died and the smoke settled low, I sat with the girl in our usual corner. She hugged her knees, her whole posture begging to disappear into the stone.

"I cannot take this anymore," I said. My voice came out harder than I meant, slicing through the silence.

Her eyes flicked toward me, wary. "Take what?"

"This. The fences. The machines. Being worked like animals and dumped in the dirt when they are done with us. You really want to rot here?"

She shifted, looking down. "I want to live. That is enough."

"No, it is not." I leaned in, lowering my voice. "You have been here longer than I have. Look around. Does anything ever change? Do you see anyone get out? Or do they just work until they drop?"

She did not answer. Her silence said everything.

"There has to be something beyond this," I pressed. "A reason. A way out. Answers. Don't you want that?"

The words sounded desperate even to me, like I was trying to convince myself as much as her.

Her hands tightened around her knees. "Want does not keep you alive. People wander. They do not come back. You think that is a coincidence?"

The words hung between us. I thought of the missing men. The old man's muttering. The cloaked woman's presence. None of it added up.

"Maybe they do not come back because they found something better," I said, though I was not sure I believed it.

Her eyes snapped to mine, sharp with anger and fear tangled together. "You do not understand. You are new. You think there is a way to beat this place, but there is not. You keep your head down, you work, you breathe, and you pray you are not next. That is survival."

"And is that enough for you?"

She opened her mouth, then closed it again. Her mask cracked for the first time.

I leaned back, softening my tone. "You are better than this place. I can see it. You have more fight than half the broken faces out here.

But you will die here if you let them keep you
caged.”

The silence stretched. Finally she whispered,
almost too soft to hear, “Damn you.”

When she looked at me again, her eyes were
not defiant. They were resigned. “If we go, we
go fast. And we do not stay long.”

That was enough.

We slipped away while the yard slept,
moving through gaps in the fence where rust
had eaten the links. The world outside was
worse than I expected. Towers of collapsed steel
leaned like broken bones. The ground was
littered with the husks of machines left to rot.
Oil stains hardened into black crust underfoot,

and the wind carried a metallic taste that coated my tongue.

The girl moved quickly, tense and alert, like a shadow ready to bolt. I followed, scanning the ruined horizon. Everything felt wrong. Too open. Too quiet.

We passed a stone wall carved with strange marks. Not letters. Jagged shapes. Symbols that did not belong to the yard. The girl froze, her face draining of color.

"What is it?" I asked.

Her voice came out as a whisper. "Rustclads."

A chill crawled across my skin. "How do you know?"

She pointed with a trembling hand. "They leave signs. Warnings. Or claims. If you see them, it means they are watching."

I looked around, the air suddenly heavy. The ruins pressed in from every direction, every shadow capable of hiding someone.

Then I saw it.

Far off, on a broken ridge where the skyline crumbled, a figure stood. A shape against the haze. Too still to be natural.

Watching.

The girl grabbed my arm hard enough to hurt. "We need to go back."

The figure remained motionless. I could not see a face. I could barely tell if it was even human. But the weight of its gaze pressed against my chest like a hand.

My mouth went dry. I wanted to argue, but no words came.

We turned back, retracing our steps through rust and ruin. Every sound felt amplified. A piece of metal clattering somewhere in the distance. The wind moaning through dead scaffolds. A long, low whistle drifting from the dark, like a signal.

By the time the yard's broken walls came into view, sweat slicked my back. The girl released my arm, but her hands still shook.

"Never again," she whispered.

I did not answer. My eyes drifted back toward the ridge.

The figure was gone.

"The yard was burning, machines collapsing, bodies falling. There was no escape. Only blood."

Chapter 10

Paranoia in the Shadows

Morning came without a sunrise, only a churn of gray smoke pressing down on the yard. I had not slept. Every time I closed my eyes, I saw that figure on the ridge, still and patient, watching from the haze.

The girl looked just as drained. She kept her hood low, her shoulders tight, moving through the crowd like someone trying to disappear before the shadows remembered her. When our eyes met, she looked away quickly.

We did not speak. Not about what we saw. Not about how close we had come to something we could not name.

Workers shuffled around us with the same dead rhythm as always, their bodies obeying a routine their minds could no longer fight. The stink of oil and sweat hit harder than before. I fell into step beside her, letting the weight of steel and the endless slam of machinery numb my nerves.

But it pressed against my thoughts until I could not keep it in.

I leaned closer. "You saw it, right? The figure."

Her jaw tightened. She didn't meet my eyes. "Shut up."

"I just need to know," I started.

"Shut up," she snapped again.

The sharpness in her voice cut through the clatter. A worker nearby turned his head, staring for a long moment before slipping back into his routine. My stomach twisted. One wrong word in here, and rumors spread like blood in water.

My hands kept moving. Metal in. Metal out. Hammer down. But my mind stayed out there in the wasteland, fixed on the ridge where that figure stood.

By midday, whispers had begun weaving through the work hall, slipping between hammer strikes, crawling under the belts, refusing to be drowned out.

"The Rustclads near the fences," someone muttered two rows over.

"Scouts," another voice hissed. "Sentries testing the ground."

More murmurs followed, spreading like infection.

A worker behind me whispered, "The Rustclads don't come unless the marks change."

Another worker snapped at him, "Quiet."

But fear broke the man open. "They scout first. They watch for weeks. They study the camps. They test the fences. If they are close, someone told them where to look."

The girl's hands trembled as she worked. She slammed her hammer harder, trying to hide the shake in her arms.

When the shift finally ended, I caught her elbow before her knees could give out. I guided her toward the outside yard, but the air offered no relief. Smoke and dust clung to the sky like a lid clamped over the world.

She finally spoke. Her voice was low and ragged. "You do not understand. If the Rustclads were that close, this yard is already marked. They will come when they are ready."

My chest tightened. "What do they want?"

She stared past me with eyes that had already seen too much. "People. Supplies.

Anything they can use. It does not matter. They take. And no one stops them."

Cold iron settled in my gut.

I wanted to believe otherwise. To convince myself that what we saw was only a shadow in the haze, a trick of distance. But the fear in her voice told me the truth.

And later, as the yard slipped into uneasy silence, I couldn't shake the feeling that somewhere beyond the broken fences, eyes were still fixed on us.

Watching. Waiting.

Chapter 11

The Old Man Returns

The yard was quieter than usual that night, though the machines still rattled somewhere in the distance. The air carried the weight of whispers again, the kind that cling to the back of your throat. People spoke less now, their eyes avoiding one another as if conversation itself might draw something out of the dark.

I sat against the wall, bone tired, when I saw him.

The old man.

The same one who had stolen the newspaper. The same one who had grabbed my sleeve and spat warnings about the Eyes. He shuffled out of the shadows like a piece of the yard had broken loose and decided to walk. His rags hung off him like rotting skin, his wiry beard matted with grease, his eyes hollow and bright all at once.

Several workers turned away immediately. Others stared at the ground, pretending he did not exist. His presence was a bad omen, and everyone felt it.

He saw me, and his cracked lips pulled into something that might have been a smile if there had been any warmth left in him.

"You are still here," he muttered. His voice rasped like sand grinding inside a metal pipe. "Didn't think you would last this long."

The girl stiffened beside me. Her fingers dug so hard into her sleeve that her knuckles turned white.

I cleared my throat. "Where have you been?"

The old man chuckled, a sound that made the hairs on my arms rise. "Places you do not want to see. Places you should not walk into unless you have nothing left to lose."

He leaned closer, his eyes flicking across the yard as if expecting something to lunge from the shadows.

"They do not vanish, you know," he whispered. "The missing —They are taken."

Cold crept down my spine. "Taken by who?"

He wet his cracked lips, revealing teeth that looked chewed down to stubs. "Out there. Beyond the fences. They come when the machines drown the screams. They drag the unlucky into the ruins, into the camps. They don't kill right away. Killing is too easy."

The girl spoke sharply, her voice low and firm. "You are full of it."

The old man's eyes snapped to hers, startlingly sharp for a moment. "Am I? You think I do not know? I have seen it. I have been there. Escaped once. They keep the strong. They break the weak. Strip you down until you are nothing but bone and obedience."

He turned back to me, pupils wide and wild. "You will see soon enough. They always come.

The fences do nothing. The machines do nothing. They will walk right through all of it."

I swallowed. "If you escaped, why come back?"

His laugh softened. It almost sounded tired. "Maybe I never left. Maybe I have been here the whole time. Maybe that is the trick."

He smiled again, but it looked wrong, like a memory that had been crushed and then forced into the shape of a grin. The girl grabbed my arm and pulled me to my feet, her jaw tight.

"Ignore him," she said. "He wants you rattled. That is all he has left."

We walked away, but his muttering followed us into the night. Broken warnings scraped the air, blending with the rising growl of the machines. His voice thinned into a whisper.

"They are coming. They are always coming."

Later, lying on the cold ground, I stared at the ceiling of smoke and shadows while his words circled through my mind.

Taken.

Not vanished. Not swallowed. Taken.

And somewhere in the ruins beyond the fence, something waited to prove him right.

Chapter 12
The Unseen Eye

The yard didn't feel the same after the whispers began. Nothing had changed in the way it looked. The fences still sagged, the smoke still clung to the sky, and the machines still rattled through every hour. Yet the air itself felt different, heavy with a presence no one could name.

Workers moved more slowly. Their eyes drifted toward the wire when they thought no one was watching. Conversations died the moment footsteps approached. Even the clang of metal sounded sharper, like every noise carried a warning hidden inside it.

I caught myself scanning the fences instead of the gears in my hands, waiting to see a figure standing there —silent and patient. Waiting for the moment the old man's warnings would stop being warnings.

The girl noticed it too. She kept her head down and worked with a focus that looked more like panic than discipline. When she spoke, her words were tight and clipped. A warning. A barrier. She hugged her arms close, as if holding something inside herself that threatened to break apart.

"You shouldn't have taken me out there," she said one night as we settled against the cold stone. "Now you will never stop looking over your shoulder."

Her tone carried no anger. Only exhaustion. She had seen this kind of fear before.

She was right. I could not stop.

Two shifts later I noticed something wrong along the east fence. A support post leaned at an odd angle, wires stretched outward as if something had pushed from the other side. The metal let out a faint groan, a sound like an old bone shifting. Workers moved past it without a glance, or maybe they simply refused to see it.

That same day two workers did not appear for the midday break. No announcement. No questions. No names spoken. People returned to their stations with hollow eyes.

Later, as I stepped away from the machinery,
I heard two men whispering behind a supply
crate.

"They say the old sentries are walking
again."

"Impossible. Those rigs need power. Control
lines. Someone would have to wind them."

"Then someone is. Patrols are tightening.
And if the Rustclads are nearby, everything gets
worse."

They stopped talking the second they
noticed me.

That night the yard fell into a strange hush.
Even the familiar coughing and the muttered
prayers seemed distant, swallowed by the smoke
that drifted low across the stone.

I was drifting toward sleep when the girl stiffened beside me. "Do you see that?" she whispered. Her breath trembled. The blanket quivered in her grasp.

I followed her gaze past the broken scaffolds and the husks of dead machines. At first I saw nothing. Then a faint glow flickered through the haze. A single bright flame, held high. It swayed once and vanished.

A few seconds later it rose again.

High once. Low once.

A sequence. A pattern. Intentional.

My pulse quickened. "A signal?"

She nodded, her face drained of color. "It means they are close."

As my eyes adjusted, I noticed something else. An old relay casing lay half buried near the fence, rust eating at its edges. Three words had been scratched across the metal in jagged strokes.

STRENGTH IS MERCY

My stomach tightened as if pulled by a hook.

The flame blinked again, high then low, repeating the pattern. No raid followed. No footsteps. No shouting. Only silence stretching across the ruins like a trap waiting to spring.

The dread that had been simmering for days finally settled deep inside me. The Rustclads were out there, close enough to send signals, close enough to mark the fences.

And somewhere beyond the haze, unseen

eyes watched us with a patience colder than any

steel in the yard.

Chapter 13

Signals in the Dark

The nights had been restless, but this one was worse. When the machines finally faded into their slow mechanical groans, the sudden quiet left too much room for other sounds to creep in. It felt like the yard itself was holding its breath.

A faint glow pushed against the cracks in the wall, warm and flickering. Not the cold lamps of the yard. Not the harsh glare of the work hall.

Fire.

I pushed myself upright. The girl sat near the broken window, her face tight with exhaustion and fear. She didn't turn when she spoke.

"See it?"

I moved beside her. Through the shattered pane, past the twisted shapes of dead scaffolds and half-collapsed buildings, I saw flames scattered across the horizon. Not one fire but many, spread like fallen embers across the ruins.

Some burned high. Some guttered low. All of them moved with a deliberateness that made my skin crawl.

Torches. Camps. Signals.

"They are watching," she whispered. "Marking us. Always marking us."

I wanted to tell her she was wrong, that it could have been scavengers or strangers passing through. But the words caught in my throat. After the whispers in the yard, after the old man's warnings, I knew better.

The flames shifted again. One dimmed until it was barely visible. Another flared bright enough to paint the ruins red. A pattern emerged, or maybe my fear carved one out of the chaos.

Either way, my stomach twisted.

"Why show themselves?" I asked quietly. "If they plan to take us, why not stay hidden?"

Her voice gained an edge I had not heard in days. "Because they want us afraid. You keep a dog in a cage long enough and you don't need to touch it to break it. You just rattle the bars until it tears itself apart."

Her words felt heavier than the air around us. I looked back toward the fences that had loomed over me since the day I woke here. I had thought they were meant to keep us in line.

Now I realized they were meant to keep us contained. The girl drew closer, her shoulder brushing mine, her breath sharp and cold. "If they want in, nothing will stop them. Not the fences. Not the machines. Not us."

We stayed at the window long after that. The flames across the horizon flickered like hungry eyes, each one blinking slow and knowing.

Neither of us spoke again. Sleep never came.

Chapter 14

Breaking Point

The next shift was brutal. The machines clanged louder, the air thickened with dust, and every motion felt like dragging chains through mud. The floor trembled beneath each slam of the press, a constant reminder that the yard owned every breath we took. But it wasn't the work that shredded my nerves. It was the fires.

Small pops. Distant cracks. Little noises drifting in from the ruins—too faint to be explosions and too sharp to be anything else. They threaded through my thoughts no matter how hard I tried to push them away. Every flare in the dark felt like a warning meant for us.

By the time the shift ended and the workers shuffled off to their corners, the girl still hadn't said a word. Her silence felt heavier than the roar of the machines.

When we finally sank into a shadowed cut in the wall, something in me snapped.

"What is going on out there?" The words came out sharper than I meant. "The fires, the whispers, the people vanishing. You know something. You've been here longer than I have. Stop pretending you don't."

Her head snapped toward me, eyes burning. "You think I'm hiding something from you? You think I've got answers?" Her voice shook with anger and something deeper. "If I did, don't you think I would be gone already?"

I leaned forward, frustration spilling out. "But you act like you expect all of this. Like it's normal. The old man's warnings, the rumors, the fires—they're not nothing. And you don't even flinch anymore."

She shoved me hard, her palm pressing into my chest. Her knuckles were white. A metallic taste crept into my mouth.

"You think that makes me strong?" she hissed. "It doesn't." She spat the word like it poisoned her tongue. "It means I'm terrified every single day, and I've learned to bury it so I don't fall apart like everyone else."

Her voice cracked, sharp and raw.

"You want answers?" Her breath shook. "There aren't any. There's only survival. Or you end up like the ones who vanish."

Her words hit deeper than I expected. The anger in me unraveled. Something steadier rose in its place.

I lowered my voice, trying to keep it from breaking. "You've kept me alive since the moment I woke up here. You showed me how to move, how to breathe, how to keep myself from drowning. "You are the only reason I haven't lost it." I swallowed, throat tight. "I don't need every answer. I just need the truth. Even if it's ugly. Even if it's fear."

She froze. Her eyes softened, just barely, like she was letting me see behind the wall she'd held up for so long. Her hands trembled where they gripped her knees.

"You're right," she whispered. "I am afraid. Every day. And I hate that you can see it."

Something changed then—quiet, heavy, fragile. The yard still stank of rust and grease. The walls still pressed in like a cage. But for the first time, it felt like the two of us weren't standing alone in it.

Her voice slipped out again, thin and brittle. "Do you know what scares me the most? Not dying. Everyone dies here. It's forgetting I existed before this place. Forgetting what I sounded like, what I wanted. Forgetting I was ever anything other than afraid."

She shut her eyes, her voice softening to almost nothing.

"You make me remember I'm still human."

She leaned against me then—not much, just enough for her head to brush my shoulder. Her weight was light, but it steadied something deep in my chest. It wasn't comfort. It was a truce. A promise.

My hand drifted toward hers, stopping just shy of her fingers. For one heartbeat, I considered closing the distance, taking what little warmth the world had left.

But I didn't.

Not because of doubt. Not because of fear. But because she hadn't offered. If we were going to survive whatever was coming, nothing could be stolen, not even a touch.

Out in the ruins, the fires still burned. I lay awake to their distant hiss, and for the first time in days, the sound didn't feel like a countdown.

And I didn't feel entirely alone.

ACT 3: FIRE AND CHAINS

Chapter 15

Fire and Blood

After our breaking point, I did not mean to ask her name. It slipped out, like my mind was trying to grab hold of something real before everything else fell apart.

We sat against the cracked wall, our backs pressed to smoke-stained stone, the hum of the yard still echoing in our bones. She studied me for a moment before answering.

"Nora," she said. Her voice was steady, but her eyes flicked downward, as if she already regretted saying it.

I turned the name over in my head. Nora. It fit her. Hard edges wrapped around a buried softness.

"You should have a name too," she said after a moment. Her lips twitched like she almost smiled. Then she shook her head. "You look like him."

"Who?" I asked.

She didn't answer. She only whispered, "Zach. That's you now."

The name hit me like a shard of metal. Strange and sharp, but better than nothing. I nodded, and she looked relieved, like giving me a name gave her back the smallest bit of control.

The quiet didn't last.

It began with a faint sound. A low clank, like a chain being tested, followed by metal dragging on stone. Then a rhythmic hiss, mechanical and alive. Beyond the fences, gears ground and hydraulics wheezed.

Workers froze. Some whispered prayers. Others pressed trembling hands to their ears as if that would keep the noise out.

Then came the voices. Not the machines this time—voices outside the yard. Harsh, wild cries from dozens of throats, a chorus of rage that sounded like it had been waiting for this moment.

The fences shook. A post snapped like brittle bone. Wires screamed as they tore apart, ripping wide enough for a man to walk through.

Shadows swarmed through the breach.

The Rustclads poured in.

They came with blades, clubs, torches, chains—anything that could kill or burn. Their faces were smeared with ash and grease, eyes wide with frenzy. Their bodies were wrapped in scraps of hammered metal. They fell upon the yard like wolves unleashed.

Screams cut the air open. Workers scattered, but there was nowhere to run. I saw one man dragged down and beaten until his skull cracked open. Another had his throat cut, blood spraying across the dirt before his body was hauled away like trash.

Nora grabbed my arm. "Move."

We ran, weaving between broken machines, trying to stay low. But a figure lunged from the smoke—a man with a jagged blade and a snarl twisted across his face.

He swung for my head.

I ducked and snatched a rusted pipe off the ground. I swung, wild and desperate. The crack of bone sliced through the chaos. Warm blood splattered up my forearm, the smell of iron hitting my nose.

He crumpled, but he was not finished. He clawed for Nora, dragging her down, his blade flashing toward her throat.

"Die!" I roared, driving the pipe into his face. Once. Twice. Again. The sounds were wet and ugly—bone giving way, teeth snapping loose. He gurgled, but I didn't stop. I kept smashing until his skull collapsed and his hand slid off her wrist.

Blood streaked across Nora's cheek. She scrambled back, panting hard, staring at me like I had become something else. Maybe I had. I saw fear in her eyes, fear and the cold recognition of a monstrous thing born from survival.

More shadows charged us. I swung the pipe again, striking one across the jaw so hard his teeth scattered across the dirt. Another grabbed my shoulder, snarling, and I jammed the pipe into his gut until he folded over, wheezing. I kicked him aside and spat blood from my mouth.

"Come on!" I screamed, throat raw, hands slick with red. "Come on if you want more!"

That was when the machines came.

The ground shuddered, a deep vibration that rolled beneath the chaos. Searchlights cut through the smoke, beams sweeping the battlefield. Hulking shapes lurched forward—rusted frames that looked like war relics dragged back from the grave. Gears screamed as they moved, their heavy arms swinging iron bars that crushed bodies into pulp. Jets of flame burst from their shoulders, turning men into burning silhouettes.

But the Rustclads didn't break. They swarmed the machines, climbing like insects, jamming hooks and blades into the gaps in their armor. One machine fell in a burst of sparks, its joints buckling under the weight. Another's searchlight flickered and died as a chain wrapped around its head and dragged it to the ground.

The air reeked of burning oil and cooked flesh.

Nora screamed my name. "Zach!"

I grabbed her hand, and We ran, but we did not get far.

Hands slammed into my back, dragging me down. My face smashed into the dirt. The pipe was torn from my grip. I kicked and fought, but more bodies piled on, boots thudding into my ribs, fists crushing my jaw.

"Rustclad trash!" I spat, choking on blood.

Beside me Nora screamed as they pinned her down, her wrists twisted behind her back.

Rough cords bit into my arms. We were dragged across the ground, bound like animals, pulled past fire and wreckage. The yard we had known—our endless prison of smoke and iron—was nothing but flames and ruin now.

The last thing I saw before smoke swallowed everything was one of the sentries still standing, its chestplate burning, gears grinding uselessly as a Rustclad hacked at its knee with a saw.

Then the darkness closed around us, and we were gone, hauled into the night. My world shrank to the taste of smoke and the bite of ropes, and everything else blurred away.

Chapter 16

Dragged Into the Dark

The world blurred into smoke and dirt as they dragged us through the wreckage of the yard. My face scraped over broken stone and twisted metal until every breath was dust and iron. Each pull left fire along my skin, rust grinding hard between my teeth. Nora stumbled beside me, her bound wrists yanked forward by rough hands. I tried to reach for her, but a boot pressed down on my spine, grinding until stars burst behind my eyes.

They hauled us out of the only place we had known, out into the dark beyond the fences. Flames swallowed the yard behind us. Ahead stretched ruins I had never seen—jagged outlines of collapsed buildings, skeletal frames of machines sinking into the earth. Some leaned at impossible angles, frozen mid-collapse like monuments to a world that had died screaming.

The Rustclads dragged us through it all, their torches cutting wild arcs through the haze. Their laughter was sharp and jagged. Some barked at each other in a guttural slang I couldn't follow. Others hissed tuneless songs under their breath, eerie things that made the hairs on my neck rise. Nora's jaw clenched, and I knew she heard it too.

They weren't just killers. They relished it.

At last, the dragging stopped.

We were shoved into a clearing—if the word even fit. Broken trucks and bent scaffolds ringed the space, their skeletal frames twisted into makeshift barricades. Fires burned in barrels and in pits carved into the earth, throwing shadows across walls of smashed metal hammered into crude shelters. The stench was suffocating: smoke, sweat, blood, and rot.

Nora pressed close when they dumped us on the ground. I felt her shaking. My arms burned from the ropes, but I shifted until my shoulder touched hers. She looked at me, and for that moment she was not guarded or fierce. She was simply afraid.

The Rustclads did not kill us, not yet. They circled, taunting, tossing scraps at our feet and laughing at our silence. One leaned close enough that I could smell the grease in his hair and the copper on his breath. He spat on my cheek and snarled something I couldn't understand. The others roared with laughter.

Then, just as suddenly, the noise began to die.

The silence spread quickly, contagious, like a sickness rolling through the crowd.

It started subtle. A few Rustclads stopped jeering and straightened. Others fell still as if a signal had passed through them. One by one, the rowdy chaos drained away until the entire camp was hushed, every eye turning toward the same place.

The firelight bent strangely across the clearing, shadows stretching long and narrow. From deeper in the encampment came a sound—deliberate and steady.

Boots against gravel.

Slow.

Unhurried.

The Rustclads parted like a tide. Even the flames seemed to bow lower, their shadows crawling back as if they, too, feared what approached. Heads lowered. None dared laugh now.

Nora's breath hitched. My chest tightened. Whoever was coming didn't need to raise his voice. The silence alone carried his authority.

The steps grew closer. Heavy. Certain. The firelight reached outward, flickering across the outline of a figure at the edge of the clearing.

The leader.

I couldn't see his face yet. Only the broad shoulders, the glint of metal at his side, and the way every Rustclad stood straighter, as if the air itself required it.

He paused, letting the silence thicken until it felt like a weight on my spine.

Then he stepped into the light.

And in that moment, I understood something cold and simple:
The yard had been a cage.
But this place, and this man, were the predators waiting outside the bars.

"This wasn't survival. It was a machine built on fear."

Chapter 17
The Camp

The march through the ruins ended in firelight. The Rustclads drove us forward with shoves and curses, dragging us over broken streets and shattered walls until the dark opened into something worse: a sprawl of tents, fires, and cages stitched together from whatever the land had left behind. Metal, wood, torn canvas, barbed wire. All of it pressed into a shape that was less a village and more a wound cut into the earth. The whole place pulsed as if it had been carved out of the night for the sole purpose of feeding on us.

The camp stank of smoke, sweat, and rot. Fires burned in barrels and pits, throwing jagged shadows across the faces that gathered to watch us stumble in. Men and women with cracked teeth and scarred skin stared at us with the same hungry shine in their eyes. Some laughed. Some spat. But every gaze held the same thought.

Prey.

Their jeers blended into a low growl that made my skin crawl.

Nora pressed close, her shoulder brushing mine. She gripped my sleeve, not out of fear, though she had every reason to be afraid, but out of defiance. She would not let them see her break.

The Rustclads were not chaos. That was the first thing I noticed. The fires burned in straight rows, not scattered. The tents formed narrow paths beaten into the dirt, each one guarded. The cages were aligned with grim precision, filled with faces hollowed by hunger and exhaustion. Even the suffering had been arranged.

A rhythm ran through the place. Voices barked orders. Fighters sharpened blades beside the fires. Children; filthy, thin, hollow-eyed carried scraps from tent to tent. This wasn't madness. It was control. Brutality shaped into routine.

One of the Rustclads shoved us down near a cage. He was tall and broad; a strip of leather tied across his forehead. My knees smacked the dirt. I caught Nora before she could fall, steadying her. She gave me a glance, quick but heavy with her lips pressed tight.

A scream tore through the air from somewhere deeper in the camp. No one flinched. No one turned. The sound fit the night the way the fires did. Expected. Ordinary. The silence that followed was worse, like the darkness itself swallowed the voice whole.

Nora's whisper barely reached me. "This isn't survival. It's a machine."

She was right. This wasn't a band of raiders scrabbling for scraps. It was an institution. Something built. Something meant to last. The yard had been a cage. This place was the butcher's block.

The Rustclads dragged another prisoner past. His face was swollen, his wrists bound tight. He tried to walk upright, but they beat him until he crawled. He did not beg. He did not scream. He already knew it would change nothing.

Some of the Rustclads carried marks across their shaved heads; brands, not ink. Symbols carved into flesh and blackened with soot. As they passed the fires, they touched the marks with their fingertips, almost reverent.

Every time they did, the flames rose higher.

Nora turned her face away, but her shoulders shook. I reached for her hand, not caring whether she pulled away.

She did not.

Her fingers locked around mine, tight enough to hurt, and I held on, clinging to the pressure like it was the only real thing left.

We sat there together in the dirt, surrounded by fire, steel, and eyes that promised nothing but pain, waiting for whatever came next.

"His whimpers thinned until silence swallowed him."

Chapter 18
Chains Within Chains

Morning in the camp was worse than night. The fires had burned down to smoldering heaps, leaving behind smoke that clung to my lungs. The Rustclads stirred early, their voices sharp and guttural as they barked orders at the captives as if we were livestock.

They yanked Nora and me off the dirt before the sun rose and shoved us into a line of prisoners stumbling toward the day's work. Shackles bit into my wrists, grinding the skin raw. Each step made the straps burn deeper The air stank of grease, sweat, and rot.

The first task was hauling wood. Not clean timber, but rotted beams and broken planks dragged from ruined buildings. My shoulders burned under the weight, each movement pulling fire through my muscles. Splinters dug into my palms. Sweat made the ropes slip and rasp. Nora carried more than she should have. Her face was pale but steady, her jaw locked. She refused to let them see her break.

By midday they pushed us to the water pits. Captives knelt beside rusted buckets, scooping sludge from black pools slick with oil and ash. Some were forced to drink it. A man gagged and convulsed for a full minute before a guard struck him down. Most just choked, only to be beaten for spilling a drop.

The punishments came as steady as the orders.

A boy no older than fifteen collapsed under his load, his legs folding beneath him. They dragged him by the hair into the center of the camp and left him without food. I watched him fade throughout the afternoon, his whimpers thinning until silence swallowed him. His bucket rolled from limp fingers and clattered, a small sound that felt like a verdict.

A woman shouted back at a guard, her voice raw and desperate. They beat her bloody in front of everyone, then dumped her against the cages. She was still breathing, but barely. Her shattered face was a warning. One eye stared past the fires like it had already given up on this world.

I kept my eyes down, but every strike, every scream, burned in my gut. I wanted to fight back, to tear their skulls open and spill their blood across the dirt, but the shackles weighed heavier than iron. They felt like death.

By nightfall, Nora and I were herded back to the pen, our bodies aching, our hands blistered. The camp pulsed with its rhythm of violence. Every cruelty delivered with precision. This wasn't chaos. There was no waste here.

The Rustclads weren't scavengers clawing for scraps. They were predators building a world out of fear. And we were caught inside it, another link in their machine.

Nora sat close beside me, her shoulders trembling. I shifted to block the eyes that lingered on her too long. Her breath shook as she whispered, low enough only I could hear.

"We're not getting out of here alive."

I curled my fists until my nails tore skin. The thought rose in me then, fierce and impossible to ignore.

Not tonight. Not like this.

I didn't answer her. Couldn't.

But inside, one idea burned hotter than the fires that lit the camp.

Not like this.

"He had not given his name. He had not needed to."

Chapter 19

Shadows of Who I Was

Sleep came like a thief. Not deep. Not merciful. Only a fall into blackness because my body had nothing left to hold on to.

The darkness did not last.

I was somewhere else. The air was sterile and crisp, humming with polished machines. No rust. No fire. No screams. Light glinted off marble floors and glass walls so clean they seemed unreal. Men and women in dark suits moved with perfect precision, their steps silent, their eyes colder than steel.

I was one of them.

A reflection rippled in the glass. I lifted a hand to my hair, expecting grime or scars. Instead I saw a neatly cut style, a sharp suit, and a silver pin on my lapel. Power clung to me like a second skin. I looked certain. I looked like someone who belonged here.

And yet anger moved beneath the surface, a memory rising like smoke.

Voices echoed, my own voice among them.

"You cannot keep them beneath you forever. They deserve better. All of them. Do you not see the rot crawling through us?"

Faces turned toward me, unimpressed or disgusted. Some smirked. Others scoffed. But one face stayed fixed in my mind: a man in the corner, lips thin, eyes hard as stone. He leaned to whisper in another man's ear, and both of them smiled like wolves.

Then came the hands.

They held me down as a needle pressed into my skin. My blood turned to fire. Voices murmured above me, flat and final.

"Wipe it clean. Throw him down with the filth he cares so much about. Let him rot there. If instinct rules men, instinct will ruin him."

Someone laughed. A hand wiped my face as if erasing a stain.

I tried to scream, but the memory shattered.

I woke choking on dust. Nora was beside me, pale in the firelight, her eyes darting to the shadows that ringed us. Our wrists were still raw from the ropes. The Rustclads stood guard around the pen, their torches flickering low.

The silence pressed harder than the noise ever had.

Then came the sound. Boots on gravel. Heavy. Deliberate. Each step was measured, like a hammer counting down fate.

The Rustclads shifted. Some lowered their heads. Others straightened like soldiers. Every laugh and sneer vanished.

I felt him before I saw him.

Authority. Presence.
A weight that did not need shouting to announce itself.

He stepped into the firelight. Tall and broad, wrapped in worn leather and steel plating. His hood shadowed most of his face, but his eyes caught the flames, sharp and intelligent, nothing like the wild stares of the men around him. A blade hung at his side, welded from salvage but polished with care.

He stopped a few feet from us and let the silence stretch until it hurt. Nora trembled against my arm, but she did not look away.

Finally he spoke. His voice was low, calm, and colder than anything I had ever heard.

"You fought," he said. His gaze fixed on me. "I can smell the blood on your hands. Not many survive their first raid. Fewer still stand back up after."

My throat was dry, but I forced the words out. "You killed them. You slaughtered them like animals."

He tilted his head, almost amused. "Animals? No. Animals kill to eat. My people kill to live. There is a difference."

The calm in his voice cut deeper than rage ever could.

His gaze slid to Nora, then back to me, sharper than a blade.

"You carry two names," he said. "The girl calls you Zach, but I know better."

He leaned closer, and the firelight revealed scars at the corner of his mouth and flecks of gray in his beard.

"Jonathon Steelle. That was the name they gave you before they burned it from your skull."

The name hit like a fist. Something in me recoiled, grief, recognition, and a flash of memory I could not catch. The ropes cut deeper as I strained against them, not knowing if I wanted to break free or collapse.

He straightened and turned. The Rustclads parted for him, silent and reverent, as he walked back into the shadows.

He did not give his name.
He did not need to.

His words dragged behind him like chains.

Jonathon Steelle.

A symbol flashed behind my eyes, not a full memory, just a shape. A silver and black flag unfurling. A circle split by a rising line. Etched into metal. Raised above a hall bright with glass and marble.

My breath caught.

The image vanished, but the echo of it clawed at me.

I had worn it once.

A name I did not remember, but one that refused to stay buried. And if that man had tugged a thread loose, everything I thought I was about to unravel.

"I was left broken in the dirt, empty and burning. And
she was gone."

Chapter 20

Chains of Fire

The name echoed long after he vanished into the shadows.

Jonathon Steelle.

The syllables pressed behind my eyes like a key grinding into a lock I could not find. I mouthed it silently, but the sound did not belong to me. It felt hammered into my skull, cold and foreign. Zach was the name that mattered, the name Nora had given me. This other one dragged behind it a weight I was not strong enough to lift.

I did not have time to wrestle with it.

Rough hands tore me off the ground. Another pair seized Nora, wrenching a scream out of her that ripped straight through the camp. She fought like she meant to tear their throats out, kicking, clawing, and twisting violently enough that two Rustclads had to pin her arms just to keep hold of her.

"Don't touch her!" I lunged forward, ropes cutting deep, skin splitting under the strain. Blood leaked warm down my wrists. They didn't care.

They never cared.

The leader stepped into the firelight again, calm and composed as if he had expected every reaction. His gaze locked on me, dark and steady.

"You feel it now," he said. "The pull of who you were. Zach is the mask. Jonathon is the truth."

"I don't know you," I spat, breath shaking. "I don't know any of this."

A faint smile tugged at his mouth it was sharp, cruel, and knowing.

"Not yet," he murmured. "But you will."

He lifted a hand.

The Rustclads obeyed instantly.

They dragged Nora back, her heels scraping trenches in the dirt as she fought. She screamed my name, the name she had given me, the name that meant something. Her fingers brushed my palm for a heartbeat, desperate and clinging, before they tore her away.

That sound, her panic, her fight, her fear, shredded something inside me.

I lunged again. A boot slammed between my shoulder blades and drove me face-first into the ground. A harsh weight pinned me there, grinding bone against stone. Nora's voice cut through the smoke.

"Zach!"

Then another cry.

Then another.

Then nothing.

Silence swallowed her.

I pressed my forehead into the dirt, breath shaking, fury trapped inside me like a storm sealed in steel. For the first time since waking in the yard, I felt truly powerless. Not beaten. Not bruised.

Powerless.

And that was when it hit.

Not a whisper.

Not a flicker.

A memory full and bright, burst behind my eyes like lightning splitting the dark.

I stood in a shining hall. Marble. Glass. A thousand polished surfaces reflecting the same moment. People in sharp suits watched me from elevated tiers, their arms crossed, their eyes cold.

I was shouting at them.

Not begging.

Not pleading.

Condemning.

"You cannot call us a nation if you build your world on their backs. You cannot preach strength while forcing half the people you rule to crawl."

The words were mine, but from a man I no longer knew.

A hand gripped my shoulder. A low voice murmured at my ear, almost pitying.

"You have gone too far, Jonathon."

I turned toward the voice, but his face
fractured into shadow before I could see it. The
memory splintered, cracking apart at the edges.
In my palm I held something small, cold, and
metallic, a strip of silver etched with a symbol I
could not quite form in my mind.

Then the memory snapped away like a rope
cut clean.

I was back in the camp.

Back on the ground.

Back in the firelight.

My wrists bled. My chest heaved. The taste
of smoke coated my tongue. The leader watched
me from a distance, his expression unreadable,
but his eyes held certainty.

He knew what I had seen. He knew who I had been, and he had been waiting for it..

Waiting for *me* to wake up.

The flames roared higher, their shadows stretching long like chains across the dirt.

Nora was gone.

Taken.

But this wasn't the end.

Not for me or her

And not for whoever Jonathon Steelle had once been. This would not be where our story broke.

The fires took my name, but I would rise from them. One way or another.

Volume one closes on the breath of fire, a name

reborn, and a world still chained.

AUTHOR'S NOTE

Thank you for taking this journey through the ruins with me.

Remnants: The Awakening began as a series of vivid dreams—images that refused to fade with the morning. I never expected those fragments to grow into a full world or introduce characters who would stay with me long after I woke. Zach, Nora, and the people who survive around them became more than shapes in the dark. They became voices worth following, even into the hardest places.

This book is the beginning of something larger, not just for the characters but for the world they inhabit. Their broken memories, their fears, and the fragile hope that pushes them forward all lead into the next chapter of their story. If you felt the weight of their struggle, or found yourself wanting to know what happens beyond the final page, then I invite you to continue on with them in Book Two.

Stories like this are built from moments—dreams, flashes of emotion, questions that linger. Thank you for choosing to spend your time with mine. I hope the journey left a mark, even a small one.

The world of ***Remnants*** is far from done.
And neither are the people fighting to reclaim it.

www.ingramcontent.com/pod-product-compliance
Lightning Source LLC
Chambersburg PA
CBHW050406110726
47899CB00008B/2670